Isla & Pickle

The Highland Show

Kate McLelland

Picture
Kelpies

Isla and her best friend Pickle, the miniature Shetland pony, were walking home from school when they saw a poster in the window of the village shop.

HIGHLAND SHOW
This Saturday!

Enter your animals
to find out who is

the WOOLLIEST SHEEP

the FASTEST HEN

the HAIRIEST COW

the PERFECT PONY

"We should compete in the Highland Show, Pickle," said Isla, "because you are the best pony in the world!"

Just then Isla's friend Rosie rode past on her pony, Belle.

"Are you entering the Perfect Pony competition this weekend, Isla?" she asked.

Belle's coat was smooth and sleek and she was very well behaved.

"Erm... yes," Isla replied as Pickle stole apples from the shop. "We'll be there!"

If Isla and Pickle were going to win the Perfect Pony prize,
Pickle would have to look smarter.
So Isla groomed him first thing in the morning...

and last thing at night.

Pickle would also have to trot gracefully.
So they practised in the fields, where it was very muddy...

and at the beach, where it was very slippy.

And Pickle would have to listen carefully and do as he was told.
So Dad told him to stop chewing the washing...

and Isla told him to stop chasing Farmer Jess's chickens.

Finally, the day of the Highland Show arrived.
It was even more exciting than Isla had imagined.
There were tractors, food stalls, woolly sheep,
fast hens and some very hairy cows.

BEST IN SHOW 2 P.M.

In fact, it was so busy that Isla didn't see
Pickle trotting away...

...to visit the lady on the cake stall.

And she didn't see him saying hello to
Farmer Jess and her Highland cows.

Isla found Pickle just in time for the Perfect Pony competition.
"Yuck, what is that stinky smell?" she said.

They watched Rosie leading Belle gracefully around the ring.
  Just then a big booming voice cried, "And now we have
PICKLE with his owner ISLA!"

First the judge came over to see how smart Pickle was –
and Pickle gave her a friendly nuzzle.

Next Isla told Pickle to trot around the ring. At first he listened carefully – then he stopped to say hello to the crowd.

Soon the crowd was as messy as Pickle.

Dad and Harris started to laugh, and then everyone else laughed too. Even the judge thought it was funny.

Then the announcer with the booming voice called out,
"First place in the Perfect Pony competition goes to...
BELLE and ROSIE!"

Isla was a bit disappointed, but she clapped loudly for her friends. Finally the announcer said, "And please give a special round of applause to PICKLE – the friendliest pony at the Highland Show!"

When they got home Isla said, "Pickle, you may not be the *perfect* pony, but you are my very best friend." Pickle nuzzled Isla and gave a proud *neeeiiiigh*.